LIFETIMES
by
Anne Attias

LIVING is

- Not an option
- A brief time on earth
- A journey to the end
- Involves participation, frustration and assimilation
- Is a work in progress
- Never remains the same
- Should not be taken for granted

Whilst we are here
What we hold Dear
We need to protect
And treat with respect

BEGINNINGS

Josie Louise Cramer opens her eyes. She feels confused, where is she? What time is it? Has she been asleep? What day is it? She feels a sense of déjà vu. Has she been dreaming, or is this sensation reminding her of something? Clarity hovers at the edge of her consciousness. Josie recognises her familiar home environment but realises that something important is eluding her. Tentatively, Josie thinks back to her past.

Josie remembered Craven Street where she was brought up. It was a two up two down terraced house with a scullery added onto the back. It had an outside toilet facing the coal shed in the backyard. Everybody knew each other in a tight knit community which turned out for weddings, funerals and special occasions to pay their respects.

When it snowed the neighbours would be out with shovels, salt would be put down to prevent sliding. Josie's father always told her to walk Charlie Chaplin style when it was slippery, leaning forward. Snowmen and snowballs were made. Sometimes boys would put stones inside the snowballs. There was no heating in the houses just a hearth fire to huddle round with a fireguard for safety.

Regular callers included The Rag Bone Man who gave donkey stones for creaming the steps in exchange for old clothes. The knife and scissor grinder came on his bike. Once a week the Mineral Man came selling flagons and bottles of Cream Soda, Dandelion and Burdock and other soft drinks. The Rent Man called each week carrying his money in a satchel, he walked around the neighbourhood safely.

Boys built gliders and dens, girls played with balls on the walls and skipping ropes. There were chants like "Poor Mary Sat a Weeping" and "The big ship sails on the Ali alio. Teenage boys wore drainpipe trousers, fluorescent socks and winklepicker pointed toe shoes. Their hair was shaped in quiffs like Elvis. They hung about street corners or played football in the playground located halfway up the street, fenced off all round with railings and high netting to prevent windows being smashed. Teenage girls had bouffant hairstyles and stiff petticoats, like the cast from Grease.

There were tin baths which necessitated heating water on the stove as well as pulling a lever downwards inside the fireplace for hot water. Leaving the oven door open in the kitchen, the bath was slid downstairs in front of the oven reaching to the kitchen door to the yard, filled then emptied with bowls after the bath. A light to the outside toilet was operated via the kitchen. It was risky using the toilet as it attracted enormous spiders and even with the door wide open was scary.

Nearby a builder had named streets after his children so there was Mary Street, Henrietta Street, Peter Street, George Street etc. Each street had its corner shop, some people bought on tick settling upon payday. Fruit and veg came from the green grocer, fish from the fishmonger, meat from the butcher, there were no supermarkets. There were Co-ops with membership stamp books.

Comics were popular especially when they offered free gifts which sold out immediately. Girls went for 'Bunty' and 'Judy', boys chose 'Beano' and 'Dandy'. Radio offered "Listen with Mother" beginning: "Now are you sitting comfortably? Then I'll begin." Children's tv included: Muffin the Mule, Watch with Mother series of Andy Pandy, The Wooden Tops, Rag Tag and Bobtail, The Flowerpot Men including the Weed. Saturday morning radio featured Children's Favourites and Josie had a request played for "Around the World".

At night Josie's parents would pull over the armchair in front of the living room window and they would watch:" Double Your Money" with Hughie Green, "The Army Game" with Bootsie and Smudge, "Take Your Pick" with Michael Miles, "This is your life" with Eamonn Andrews, "The Black and White Minstrel Show" where white people blackened up. On Sunday afternoon on the radio there was the Billy Cotton show with his "Waikey waikwey" call. 'Carry on' films were popular at the cinema along with big epics like South Pacific. The Gaumont cinema had an organ which moved up and down the front of the curtain before performances.

The parlour was rarely used, it had an ornate fireplace and a strip of lino running from the front door to the living room door. Josie enjoyed polishing it and sliding the duster along like a pretend skating rink. Her bedroom had a water tank above the bed, and a loft where household boxes were stored. Josie called it Casablanca and enjoyed sitting up there on top of the world. The tin bath was stored at the side of the wardrobe covered by an old curtain. Sometimes the frost and ice formed lacy curtains inside the windows.

Josie's friend Linda lived across the road, she was 5 months older so started school a whole term earlier. Shortly afterwards, some new houses with gardens were built in the countryside. Linda's family moved away as they were fortunate enough to get one. They kept in touch and exchanged visits in the summer holidays until Linda's family emigrated to Australia on the ten pound scheme.

When Josie started school, she sat at a small table and was given a tin of cards with pictures on with words underneath. She could not read or draw well and thought perhaps the other kids could. There were play areas in the classroom and friendships were formed. In the primary school everybody sat two to a table, located in rows. The teacher stood at the front with chalk and when the headmaster came in, everybody felt nervous. Josie saw him once at the local cinema with his arm around a lady. She cringed and tried to hide even at an advanced age.

In the late 1950s to support the Ban the Bomb movement, it was Beatnik era. Black clothes were worn, long V-necked pullovers, medallions, pull on leggings with a stirrup under the heel. From playing childhood games of jacks, pick up sticks, board games, etc. Josie went from a tricycle to a royal blue and turquoise two-wheeler where she drove around the neighbourhood with the boys. Traffic was light, not many families had a car, nobody had a 'phone but there was a coin operated phone box at the top of the street.

Being naughty included hiding when called in for bed. The grocer at the top of the street used a white marker pen to advertise her wares on the shop windows. Sometimes kids removed a few letters like in Apple pies with the" i" removed. They also played knocking on doors and running away. When the Salvation Army came around serenading in the street, they hid indoors. When the Army knocked for contributions, they shouted, "We're not in." It was difficult to be too bad as people would tell parents.

Josie's aunty Betty lived next door to them, so when she was in trouble she would go to her aunt for sympathy. Aunty Betty had a piano and taught Josie to play "Oh will you wash my father's shirt, oh will you wash it clean ..." She also had a lava lamp with

Trafalgar Square on one side and a fireside scene on the other. When plugged in, it made the scenes flicker. Aunty Betty married later in life and in her prime, went on adventurous holidays by ship to America, Nice and exciting destinations. Nobody had been abroad in the family before her, except Josie's father as a soldier in the war.

Young kids were given spoons of Rosehip Syrup, Viral or Cod Liver Oil for extra nourishment. As they grew, Halibut orange tablets were taken. Food was prepared daily as there were no frozen meals. Buying cakes was a luxury. Most housewives shopped almost daily, cooked and baked everything. Kitchens were too small to cater for much storage. Early fridges were bulky, but the space inside was minimal. Shelves and movable cupboards were used to store, early washing machines were only half automatic, clothes rotated around a spindle in the centre, but had to be put through a wringer, water emptied in the sink from a hosepipe.

Neighbours were friendly and had a few quirks. There was Beryl who used to bite people when she was little. Mrs Bozick who examined all the children's hair before allowing them to play with her kids. There was a bride in her white dress running up and down the street, knocking repeatedly on one of the doors. The shopkeeper's daughter Moira used to enact mini theatrical productions in her backyard, always saving the plum roles and best costume pieces for herself.

A guy called Terry used to build dens and talked about girl's privates. He later smuggled his wife to be on board a ship and was in the paper. His sister, Virginia used to wear bright lipstick and could be seen snogging at the end of the street around the corner. Mr Hurst owned a horse and waggon, sometimes he would round up the kids and drive them round the neighbourhood. Mr Gormley, we called the Hermit because he rarely surfaced, gave out polo mints to all when he did.

In 1961 Josie passed the Eleven Plus exam that entitled her to go to a grammar school. The alternative was to go to a comprehensive school. Different academic qualifications were sat in the two streams. A list of schools was provided to select from. Josie's friends chose North Manchester Grammar school, so she followed suit. Her mother felt unsure because Josie was not academic. Comprehensives offered technical choices. The school uniform was Oxford blue and gold. The compulsory hat was only abolished in later years if wearing a blazer. It was a girls' school. Detention was issued for being caught not wearing the hat. Lines had to be written in detention.

To get to school there was a special bus. Later, Josie and friends preferred to go on a public bus to see the boys en route to their school. Segregated schooling did not lead to good social skills when mixing in society. All the boys were given nicknames like Freddie, Becky, Herbert bearing no relation to reality. The boys did not speak to the girls who watched them covertly.

Gradually, bouffant hair styles were replaced by "failed Cleopatras" according to the headmistress, who resigned when comprehensive schooling was introduced. Miss Webster, the headmistress, had a favourite expression that "left something to be desired." In Domestic Science the class on duty used to take her morning coffee on a tray in the staff lift, wearing red gingham aprons and caps made in sewing lessons. Girls gave a little curtsey.

Free school milk was issued at morning break. When it rained at lunchtime pop music was played in the gym, the Shadows routines like 'Apache' were popular. Miss Cameron the PE instructor, tried to teach her girls to Tango to Billy Fury's "Jealousy" record. There was also a popular game of Pirates in the gym to cross the room without touching the floor using all the laid-out gym equipment.

Josie was only good at subjects she enjoyed. When she was not interested, she developed a tendency to daydream. Initially, Josie did well in French but when she was moved down to a lower group for French and maths, interest sunk too. She was more interested in wondering whether the little old French teacher's cardigan was on inside out.

Maths was acceptable if attention was paid during demonstrations. There were logarithms charts, no calculators or slide rules, no multiple choice answers. Brain power was required. Josie did not like the mathematical problems. English composition was Josie's favourite subject, followed by art. The art teacher would describe a painting in detail and leave everybody to interpret her brief.

TV shows included Juke Box Jury where Janice Nichols from Birmingham used to say: "Oi'll give it five" and "Ready Steady Go" with Cathy McGowan, and "Top of the Pops." Sunday afternoon radio featured Alan Freeman's "Pick of the Pops". Pirate Radio ships sprung up, the most famous being Radio Caroline with DJs becoming famous playing nonstop pop music. Music moved on from Rock n Roll to Tamla Motown then along came the Beatles.

Fashions had gone from Dr Zhivago maxi coats, fur trims, to "Cleopatra" starring Elizabeth Taylor and Richard Burton. Hemlines went down to maxis, up to minis, midis, then to hot pants or fashionable shorts. From ringlets, hair was straightened with an iron. Geometric haircuts by Vidal Sassoon were in vogue, Mary Quant and Biba were the fashionistas. Carnaby Street, London was the shopping 'in' place.

Bonfire Night was popular. Before the event kids would go around the neighbourhood collecting wood and stuff to burn. Kids would make a guy and wheel him about asking: "Penny for the guy." Guards would be posted on the bonfire, each street hoping to be the last to light up. Boys threw bangers and rip raps like mini radiators around. Girls went for Roman Candles, sparklers and pretty displays like Snowflakes. Treacle toffee would be handed out. Diehards would bake potatoes in the embers.

In free time Josie and the neighbourhood kids used to go to all the area parks or walk to the city centre and back. They would congregate on the corner shop steps to chat. One of the guys, Paul Ashworth wrote poetry. The newsagent's son Graham would self-harm and show off his wounds. He wanted to go into the army. Nobody asked him why he hurt himself regularly. There was acceptance all round. Protestants were Proddy Dogs, Catholics were Tom Cats and Jews were Jew Drops. There were no foreigners around and to see a black face was rare.

In those days nobody thought of accusing the dustbin men of breaking and entering because if people were not quick enough to open their backdoors, a face would appear over the top with a stick to open the door and pull the bin out. There was one bin per family which contained all the waste. The window cleaner left his ladders in Josie's backyard when he went for lunch. His sister Mavis collected for him on Friday evenings with her hair in rollers tied up in a chiffon scarf.

Every Shrove Tuesday there was a parade of floats in the city centre, organised by students with proceeds in aid of charity. They sold Rag Rag booklets and sometimes kidnapped spectators to ransom for charity. Bands played as they marched, streamers were sold and waved. Pancakes were the culinary treat.

Whit Week had parades with crowds lining the city centre streets. There were two parades: one day for the Protestants, another for Catholics. Both had brass bands, girl guides, boy scouts, school uniforms, floral displays, banners. One of the highlights was when bandleaders threw their batons in the air and always caught them.

At the end of the street there were the fields consisting of a big wide plateau bordering Salford and Cheetham, Manchester. At various times gypsies would park on it, before being moved on by the police. Salesmen carrying fully laden suitcases or gypsies would knock on doors selling things. Josie's mother always brought some lucky heather or pegs, she did not want to be cursed.

Several times a year the fair would park on the fields at the bottom of the street attracting crowds from near and far. Josie stood on her doorstep watching the crowds stream down the street, listening to all the latest pop music. She knew the words to many songs better than her school lessons. At night she would secretly listen to Radio Luxemburg under the bedclothes and joined Jimmy Saville's Teens and Twenties Club. Occasionally, there would be fights at the fair and the wounded would limp back up the street sometimes bleeding. Mostly, it was good and finished at a reasonable hour. Everybody knew the regular crew. Josie enjoyed the chairoplanes then the waltzers where guys spun the chairs.

Social life consisted of ice skating at Derby Street Ice Rink, cinema matinees at the Rialto or Bounty cinemas which were called the fleapit, dancing at Chiltern's School of Dancing where Max Bygraves singing "You need hands" was regularly featured for the Barn Dance, there was the Gay Gordon etc. In the summer Josie went swimming at Cheetham baths with the kids. All these activities were unsupervised by the adults and there was no money for transport, so she walked everywhere.

Whilst watching "Mutiny on the Bounty" once, a minor fire broke out and Josie was evacuated from the Rialto cinema midway. There were usually two films, Newsreel, Pearl & Dean advertisements, plus trailers, each session. Ices and refreshments were served from portable trays carried by assistants. Sometimes there was money for chips on the way home.

Josie's mother took her to Oldham for shoes, a factory mill showroom called Silvana for special clothes. Her mother knitted and sewed most of her clothes. Family outings included Lime Park for a treat on two buses; and Buxton where they paid to enter the gardens. Mosley Street bus station provided the transport. There were also days out to local seaside resorts like Blackpool and Southport. Local outings included regular trips to Heaton Park where they often had to queue for buses. There was a little train inside the park to take people around. Crowds visited weekly.

One of the two Maureens who lived in the street was a big fan of Cliff Richards. Josie used to dance to his records in Maureen D's front room. She used to pretend to be part of the backing group. Josie and Maureen got Dansette record players which played 45s and 33s long players. Up to ten singles could be loaded in one go and would drop down in rotation. There were singles, extended players and long players in sleeves. Everybody watched Cliff's movies: 'The Young Ones' and 'Summer Holiday'.

Josie remembered hiding in the classroom stationery cupboard lunchtimes with her friend Rose to avoid going outside. In the third year a new girl arrived called Vicky, who sat adjacent to Josie. It was the start of a lifelong friendship. Vicky used to hide behind the piano in music lessons reading. The musical listening to The Peer Gynt Suite, The Nutcracker etc. was good, but the quavers were not too successful. On a school classical concert outing, Josie and Rose had to report to the headmistress for giggling when the enormous cymbals clashed unexpectedly. The music teacher hissed that she was sitting next to a pair of fools.

Youth clubs were attended locally featuring soft drinks, table tennis, weekend dances. It was a chance to meet local boys, but mainly consisted of girls dancing together and boys watching from the sides. Soft drinks were available. Joining a band or doing sporting activities only attracted the hard core. Mostly Josie went to see who was there, hear some music then walked home, she often did not take her coat off. A boy who resembled George Harrison was highly sought after.

Next to the Rialto cinema was a club called The Whisky A Go Go where The Beatles made one of their early appearances. Josie hung about waiting to see them but had to return home at bedtime before they arrived. A neighbour with connections got tickets to see the Beatles at the Apollo, fourth row from the front. Josie's picture was in the paper next day. The media made girls scream long before there was any sign of the group. Nurses were on standby for fainting girls. Boys had Beatle haircuts.

City Centre clubs sprang up where famous groups appeared. People walked around with their coats on all evening. Josie went to The Twisted Wheel which often featured: Rod Stewart, Long John Baldry, Julie Driscoll, Spencer Davis, John Mayall Blues Band. It had a DJ in one part, live music in another, featuring a series of rooms on various levels with wheels interspersed instead of window frames. In addition, there was the Jungfrau, The Oasis, the Cavern, Time and Place where George Best hung out, Annabelle's, Tiffany's plus popular coffee bars like the Cona and Mogamba.

Bell bottomed trousers were fashionable. Josie's mum added inserts to widen the flares which were much admired. Sometimes Josie would dance on stage with her friends. Most clubs were in the cellars of old buildings and offered free nights midweek. The Oasis had purple lighting which highlighted anything white including dandruff. The scene split into mods and rockers. Mods drove scooters flying long pendants, and wore the latest fashions. Rockers rode motorbikes and wore leathers. Some seaside resorts came to blows because of the differences.

Josie managed a ride round the city centre on a scooter, holding on to the driver's Parka coat. Hanging around outside The Twisted Wheel she saw Ike and Tina Turner go in. Once she met a member of The Zombies group and ended up snogging. Famous footballers and visitors would often visit the club when in town. She met Dave Berry at The Oasis. New Century Hall had occasional dances featuring Herman's Hermits and other top names. It also had ballroom dancing sessions which did not appeal to Josie and friends. They went to Belle Vue occasionally which featured two ballrooms and a revolving stage.

Belle Vue Zoological Gardens was a large zoo, amusement park, exhibition hall complex and speedway stadium. **Belle Vue**, Manchester, England, opened in 1836. The brainchild of John Jennison, the gardens were initially intended to be an entertainment for the genteel middle classes, with formal gardens and dancing. It **opened in**: June 1836 in Gorton. It started from humble beginnings, but by its heyday **Belle Vue** was Manchester's biggest and best-loved tourist attraction.

On 24 Mar 2014 a plaque was also unveiled at the Showcase cinema on Hyde Road, where the attraction stood before it closed in 1977 and was later **demolished**. Once the entertainment capital of the north, **Belle Vue** attracted around 2m visitors a year in its heyday. As well as the zoo, it boasted a fairground, circus, dance halls and speedway stadium and hosted performances by the likes of the Rolling Stones, Jimi Hendrix and Led Zeppelin in its later years.

Belle Vue was ahead of its time. It had a big zoo, gardens, fair, boxing, dog racing, conference hall, ballrooms, speedway, stadium, amusements. For a nominal amount families could enter. There were elephant rides, a mini train circulating the grounds, refreshments, the Snake House, the Monkey House, always plenty to do. Families queued in lines. There was nothing like it, it was a forerunner of the modern theme parks.

Most years Josie's family managed a week's holiday at the seaside. Her dad had to take set leave in August. Different factories and Works took turns to close. Sometimes Rose accompanied Josie. The furthest they got was Torquay where it rained the whole time. Other trips were to Scarborough, Rhyl, even Llandudno. They usually travelled by train. Some boarding houses kept people outside during the day.

When the currency changed from Pounds shillings and pence to decimalisation, it alarmed people, especially the elderly. Josie never got the hang of metric measurements. When Josie visited Beamish on a coach trip, she was amused to see the Bank there showing old currency as an exhibit. The English had been very set in their ways. English cuisine was normal, international food was considered as foreign muck.

Women did not usually go into bars alone. If they had a drink out they often chose Babycham or Cherry B. They waited for men to ask them to dance or invite them out. Girls sprayed hair lacquer, used Body Mist deodorant spray, pan stick makeup, bright pink or orange lipstick, pale eye shadow and eye liner. Stiletto shoes tended to get stuck in pavements and marked dance floors. There were platform shoes, knee length white laced boots. Josie's mother disapproved of eye shadow, she felt only common girls wore it. Josie used to put it on when she went out and wipe it off before the returned.

Manchester city centre as not pedestrianised. There was a cinema on market street with a poor reputation, opposite the famous Kardomah cafe. Henry's cheap department store was in Market Street and the Manchester Evening News offices were around the corner at Cross Street. On Saturdays the city centre was thronged with people, there were no local precincts. Piccadilly bus station was part of the entertainment. An all night double fare bus service was available. Drunks and weirdos hung around.

Smoking among the young tended to be done secretly whilst babysitting or in secluded places. There was a drug called a purple heart but was only known by hearsay. Under age boozing was virtually unknown as the licensing laws were strictly adhered to. There were All Nighters, but Josie couldn't go. Embassy cigarettes offered coupons which could be collected and exchanged for goods. In those days many people smoked everywhere including restaurants.

Most houses were rented, televisions were also rented for easy maintenance and because they could be exchanged when upgrades appeared. Credit was limited and only used in desperation, usually people saved up to be able to buy something. Knitting and sewing patterns took care of clothing. Prizes were available to savers of Green Shield Stamps and the Saturday Hospital Fund which offered medical discounts and convalescence facilities. Gifts of Premium Bonds were popular with Ernie making regular draws. Saturday night was football coupon night. Josie's dad used to do Spot the Ball competitions too.

BBC2 broadcast its first colour pictures from Wimbledon in 1967. By mid 1968, nearly every BBC2 programme was in colour. Six months later, colour came to BBC1. By1969, BBC1 and ITV were regularly broadcasting in colour. It was very exciting watching programmes in colour, like the cinema.

Josie had a lady doctor which was unusual. When Josie had to go to see her, the doctor was always more interested in her prospective career than her ailments.
Once when Josie said she was unwell the doctor replied: "How can anyone feel well in this weather?" Most careers open to women were teaching, nursing, secretary, nursery, catering and factory. University with grants was available for the brainy ambitious candidates. Further education courses were often free or affordable.

Josie was friendly with Susan, the eldest girl of a Catholic family of five who lived up the street. Although Susan was a few years older, they hung around together.

One evening whilst loitering around the Waltzer on the fair, Josie fell through the boards of the roundabout. She was helped out by staff, surprised but unhurt.

Two boys were regulars around the fair, one called John and one called Jimmy who looked like Keith Richards of the Rolling Stones. Susan fancied Jimmy. For her sake, Josie agreed to go out with them. Everybody caught the bus to Regent Road, Salford where the fair had moved. On the way home to Josie's surprise, John kissed her. She was too young to appreciate the moment and never went out with him again.

Meanwhile Susan went to the Catholic high school on Tetley Lane. Adjacent to the school was North Salford school for boys. Susan met Chris through school, he walked her home. He was Protestant and a bit older than Susan. They became an item and she became pregnant in her teens. Neither family were pleased. Until the pill came along, the risk of unwanted pregnancy with the accompanying shame and stigma often prevented illicit sex. Susan gave birth to a girl and promptly got pregnant again the following year to a big bouncing boy. The couple had a quiet wedding and have remained happily married ever since.

Old Mrs Davies died and her adult son Harry who was left in the house, applied for a high rise apartment. He obtained one in a new block in Silk Street, Salford, near to town. Harry offered to take a few neighbours to view it so when Josie called for him, she found he had fallen asleep and burnt his kettle which had been whistling away unattended. It was the first apartment Josie had seen with panoramic views, a long corridor with rooms leading off. It seemed large and impersonal.

Whilst America struggled with Vietnam, Josie's world was abruptly changed forever in the Sixties when there was a nationwide rehousing programme. Compulsory purchase orders appeared everywhere. Whole communities were demolished to be replaced by concrete jungles called modern council housing estates with tiny windows, and tower blocks of flats. Displaced citizens were given up to three offers of new accommodation or compensated if they had purchased their homes. Overspill estates sprung up on the outskirts of city perimeters.

Josie accompanied her mother on a bus ride to its terminus to view the area of the first offer. They passed sheep and cows in fields, went down a stretch of motorway and Josie's mother was horrified. The flat was in a tower block in the countryside which was refused immediately. They caught the same bus back. Doctors letters were called for, forms submitted and together with aunty Betty, Josie's mother managed to get a tenth floor flat in north Manchester, with a bus route to town and local shopping areas. Aunty Betty got an eighth floor flat across the road and they could wave from their kitchen windows.

Gradually the neighbours scattered. Houses were boarded up or vandalised. The area became a haunted deserted ghost town. Friends and neighbours vanished without trace never to be seen again. Suddenly, Josie's family were entombed in a box with a steel cage lift that didn't always work. They neither saw nor knew their new neighbours for years. It was a silent, isolated world. Being unable to open a front door to check the weather, it was irritating to reach ground level to discover an umbrella was needed.

It was too far to walk to the shops or town. Josie's father cut across a valley to walk to the new library at the Abraham Moss Centre, when he could spare time at weekends. As the block of flats was on a hill, the wind blew strongly. In the winter the slope approaching the block was slippy. Outings to pay the papers or get bits of shopping needed planning. In an instant the family became anonymous. Some mothers trapped in similar environments took Valium. The Rolling Stones had a hit about "Mothers Little Helpers."

There was a laundry on the ground floor which was partially manual. Each flat had an oblong storage cupboard on the ground floor. At first the area was sought after and well kept. As time progressed building defects were discovered. Upper floors became damp and mouldy, a health hazard. Wallpaper peeled and stained. A new mixture of residents was allowed into the tower blocks. Young people released from care institutions mixed with families. Cleanliness and pride in the appearance of the property disintegrated into vandalism and graffiti.

Josie had left school. There was a leavers disco with Vicky's boyfriend fronting a live group who got everybody dancing. Vicky and an accomplice put band name stickers around all the toilets. Everybody was up dancing and the school hall was dressed appealingly. It was a happy event, the last time most of the pupils saw each other.

For the GCE certificates, a ceremony called Speech Day took place at the Free Trade Hall, where everybody endured civic speeches, hymns and had to remember to lift their seats up and down gently for the presentation. Finally, Josie was free and uncertain what to do. A local pharmaceutical supply company offered her a job making up orders. It was staffed mainly by married women. Long aisles of shelving stretched endlessly. Josie was given orders and a basket, she had to locate the items from thousands of products. Despite helpful assistance, Josie's mindset could not grasp the locations.

Whilst Josie's school friends had careers in mind, some stayed on to do 'A' level GCEs to go to university, Josie was unfocused. After talking to friends, Josie went with her mother to Salford Technical College to register for a commercial course entailing: elementary accounts, commerce, computer studies, typing, shorthand and French. It would give her flexible modern skills to be able to earn a living whilst she decided where her future lay.

When Josie went to College the first day, it was in the process of moving to new premises. She had to help to unpack desks and chairs, set up the new classrooms, the lifts in the building were not working. The new College was still being built.
The new class was already split into cliques leaving Josie, a girl called Lizzie and a boy. Josie and Lizzie immediately sat together at opposite ends of a desk and became lifelong friends. The boy who wanted to be a reporter, had to make do.

Lizzie had gone to a Catholic girls' grammar school with nuns. She and Josie had similar qualifications and were so competent at French dictation, they both wrote down all the punctuation instructions as well. Lizzie's mum lived across the main road in a tower block, also on the tenth floor. One time when Josie and Lizzie decided to wag a lesson, they put up an umbrella on a sunny day, thinking if her mother looked out of the window, she would not recognise them walking along. Without intention, Lizzie and Josie turned out to be virtually synchronised in their actions and reactions, so were nicknamed The Beverley Sisters, although they did not look alike.

It was very exciting for both girls to be surrounded by boys. They had nicknames for students such as Blue Beard, Green Jumper, Strong man who couldn't open the college door) and it was fun. Josie did very well at College without really trying. She learnt to touch type on Adler and Olivetti typewriters to the tune of William Tell Overture. It would play then a formal voice would instruct "Carriage return". The class did a period on a manual typewriter then on an electric typewriter. Mistakes were blotted out using tippex paper. When carbon paper was inserted making duplicate layers, it was a real hassle to make corrections.

Meanwhile Cheetham Hill was razed, Waterloo Road shops disappeared, the prefabs along Barrow Hill Road went. Salford Brow and the area where DJ Dave Lee Travis came from disappeared. The Warden's houses were privatised and modernised. At the same time, Great Cheetham Street/Leicester Road area of Salford was also redeveloped. The entire landscape changed virtually overnight. The replacement housing looked worse in many cases. Overspill populations from other areas moved in. Some areas like Hulme with unstable crescents had to be demolished after a few years.

Eventually, St Albans Church and vicarage was demolished. The boy scouts hut went. Barrow Hill Road wasteland was turned into Alderman Rachel Finkel park featuring regular football matches. A massive urban regeneration programme took place throughout Manchester. Bathrooms with indoor toilets were appreciated.

In the holidays Josie went down to Newquay and got a job as an omelette chef. She rented a room in a Council house and saved cigarette coupons for the family there. Many people smoked Embassy and saved the coupons to be exchanged for gifts. Cigarette machines were available everywhere, most people smoked. Newquay was full of Australian surfers who swore constantly and were colourful characters. Most people did not swear in those days. There was a 9pm watershed for adult themes in the media.

Whilst enjoying the sun, sand and surfers' paradise, Josie had a good job offer which could lead to a career in the civil service. She had applied before she left and had to decide whether to choose fun or career. Reluctantly, Josie headed home. People tended to stick to a job in order to advance. Anybody who moved around a lot was viewed with suspicion. Senior titles went to mature staff members. Youngsters were trainees or apprentices. Day release or training was part of the package. Jobs were advertised in the Manchester Evening News. Often one interview was enough, and decisions were made on the spot or shortly afterwards. It was possible to chop and change jobs as the market flourished.

When Josie left school, she knew nothing practical. What use was an amoeba or spirogyra in the everyday world? She could not change a plug, knew nothing about managing finance. Careers advice at school was very hit and miss. Rose was interested in social work but ending up in teaching due to bad advice. Everything was constantly changing, but there was the need to earn a living and settle down.

Film stars changed from Doris Day to Omar Shariff and Julie Christie. Epics including Ryan's Daughter, Lawrence of Arabia, The Sound of Music, kept cinemas full. Television only had BBC and ITV with limited viewing. Coloured tv replaced black and white. Stereos changed from big pieces of furniture to small units. Cassettes and videos started to infiltrate. Amstrad computers began to replace typewriters. Courses provided information on how to use them. Telex machines were replaced by faxes.

Popular cowboy series featuring John Wayne, Clint Eastwood, Chuck Connors were replaced with detective series ranging from Dixon of Dock Green, Z Cars, later Starsky and Hutch. There were famous dramas including The L Shaped Room, dealing with topical social issues at the time. Josie's mother's favourites were Shirley Bassey and Max Bygraves. Her father liked a good male cantor like Mario Lanza.

As the Swinging 60s progressed, Manchester provided star acts including: The Hollies, Herman's Hermits, Freddie and the Dreamers, Wayne Fontana and the Mindbenders. Student concerts and dances featured all the famous acts live. Once Josie's heel snapped on her shoe, one of the Bonzo Dog Doo Dah Band tied it back on for her before their act.

At one of the Salford University dances Josie met the man who would break her heart for the first time. He was tall with curly hair, blue eyes and asked her to dance. From Padstow, Cornwall, he was a chemistry student whose father died shortly after his 21st birthday. He interrupted Josie's lecture to tell her he was going home. She never heard from him again but saw him romancing another girl at one of the dances.

Whilst on Salford University campus Josie noticed an advert for a trip to Greece. Passengers paid a set amount and would travel from Bath. It was inexpensive and seemed exciting, so Rose and Josie got fast track passports. Rose went to Liverpool and cried to get them. It seemed that some students had a van kitted out with seats and would drive to Athens and back throughout the summer vacation to make some money. Josie and Rose went down to Harold the driver's home where they stayed overnight sleeping on the lounge floor. They had a walk round Bath in the evening and admired The Crescent.

Josie and Rose had never been abroad before, so it was very exciting. Whilst the other passengers brought light luggage, naively the girls took suitcases and had no camping gear. A second driver, Fred, joined the van which set up to collect the remaining passengers all around London area. Rose and Josie sat on an old two seater bus seat fitted at the back. One of the passengers bought a bag of apples and proceeded to eat them all, one after another without offering them round. The other passengers were more worldly having travelled before.

Crossing the channel was interesting, having coffee dawn at the quayside in Belgium was fun. Rose ordered in school girl French. Driving through Austria was picturesque, waking up to mountains shrouded in mist and glowing in sunshine was a beautiful experience. Everybody except Josie camped outside the van. Josie felt nervous about insects so slept in the van.

In Germany they were amused by signs saying Autofahrt, but not amused by the policeman in green uniforms. Driving through Yugoslavia they noticed it was poor, animals sharing dwellings with residents. In Sofia, Bulgaria, they were told off by a policeman for walking on some grass. The currency changes were shared by all. One night they were parked in a wooded campsite when they heard men singing approaching, suddenly it stopped, and all went quiet. They finally arrived in Greece late one afternoon and parked at a seaside campsite where the sea felt warm and welcoming.

Josie found the light in Greece to be so dazzling, it made her eyes water. The girls were dropped off in Athens at a Youth Hostel and forgot to make arrangements for the return journey. It was busy, people were sleeping on the roof. Men were allegedly repairing the girls' showers. Girls were walking around naked. People were huddled around a television showing the **Apollo 11** Mission - **Neil Armstrong,** the first man walking on the moon. It was 1969, Josie was young, free and excited.

Josie and Rose set off for a walk in Athens, to get their bearings. It was hot, dusty, busy, bustling. Two men approached them and helped with directions, they wanted to make a date. The girls agreed to get rid of them, hurried back to the hostel and decided to go to Piraeus, the nearby port the next day to avoid the date. Josie had a Greek phrasebook ready. They got the train from Omonia Square and got a taxi to take them to an inexpensive hotel near the port. The hotel was full of seamen wearing striped trousers like deckchairs. Washing dried in minutes on the roof.

The girls set off to explore Piraeus and met Yurgos, originally from Egypt, who spoke perfect English and assigned himself to be their chaperone. He moved them from their hotel to a better one called Europa. The hotel clerk fancied Rose and when she went off on a date one night, sighed wistfully saying he had to take to drink, returning with a glass of milk.

Yurgos took the girls sightseeing in Athens. They went to the Parthenon, Acropolis Museum, Plaka old quarter, plus saw picturesque sights along the way. He bossed the girls about, introduced them to the Greek customs, a loyal friend. They met his mother at his home. He was never interested in them romantically, he was only their protector and escort.

All the shops around the port in Piraeus were arranged in segments selling the same type of product. The shoes shops were all located together, the dry goods, everything was in clusters. It was easy to walk around, everybody was friendly and helpful, apart from the hairdresser who charged the girls for a dry styling. Fashions seemed dated, but it was a family friendly place. Boat trips were advertised along the front. The girls took a boat ride to Spetses island for a few days, where there were no vehicles. They stayed in a local home, but found it too quiet, so were glad to return to Piraeus.

Every night families would parade up and down Pasalimani promenade, leading to a free dance on the end cordoned off. A male escort had to accompany females in. Yurgos took care of everything. Families would stop, wish each other good evening, offer nuts or snacks. The girls learnt a few Greek phrases and loved the ambience, the Greek music, the food. When Greeks drank Nescafe, they stirred the powder in the bottom of the cup for ages before adding the water and milk. Souvlaki was the local take away, with places offering sandwiches and toasties choosing your own fillings from display fridges.

One night a new male arrived at the dance and invited Josie to dance. She looked up and her heart fluttered, her knees felt weak and she felt like he was the only man in the world. He was tall, dark, handsome, fit, smart wearing white trousers and a fitted turquoise shirt. Unfortunately, he did not speak any English, Josie could barely speak. A tourist policeman called Vangelis came along to translate. They were introduced, Stavros was his name. Josie didn't see him again until the night she was leaving.

With limited funds dwindling, the girls decided it was time to check out return dates. To save money Rose went to the Youth Hostel in Athens alone to check for return dates. Whilst there she met a man who had a boat. He was going cruising with his friends and asked if the girls would be interested in cleaning out the boat for them, prior to the trip. The girls could stay on the boat for free. Rose came back, Josie thought it was a good idea, so they met the man who took them to the boat which was compact but comfortable. Unfortunately, it had bed bugs at night, so they slept on deck. Vangelis told the girls not to sleep outside, they could attract trouble.

The girl made a few mistakes in Piraeus. Once they innocently sat in front of a café known for prostitutes. When Josie went to the toilet, a man followed her into the room. When they wanted their hair washing and setting, the hairdresser charged them for putting their hair up dry. When they needed to buy some "pagos" (ice) for the cooler on the boat, they found some but did not have a container to put it in. When the boat man called round to check on them, Josie was stuck on the toilet constipated, the toilet door kept sliding open.

Dirty washing was accumulating so the girls found a launderette, collected their clothes in big bags and took it round. Two young men were working there and wanted the girls to leave their things. The girls needed their washing back so the four went behind the shop washing and scrubbing in a big tub, including smalls, then taking the wet washing back to dry on the boat. The men refused payment, so the girls bought them a big box of chocolates and took them round

It was time to go home. The boat man was getting ready to cruise and invited the girls along. They were not so naïve and thanked him but declined, saying they needed to go back to

England. As it was Josie's birthday, the girls arranged to meet the boat man in Athens with their luggage. He offered them a family house to use overnight before their departure. On a last walk around Piraeus, the girls popped into the dance to say goodbye to their new friends. Stavros was there, with the aid of Vangelis, he exchanged addresses with Josie, then she had to leave. They were both sad to leave Piraeus.

The boat man and friend took the girls to a fancy ice cream parlour to celebrate Josie's birthday, then they parked outside a house. The girls were assigned a bedroom and when Josie used the bathroom to clean her teeth, she noticed the two men wearing only underpants sitting on the bed. She went to tell Rose who walked calmly into the room and said: "Oh, are we sleeping somewhere else?" The men were ashamed so got up and left. The girls slept with a chair under the door handle. Early next morning they were unceremoniously dumped outside.

After a long uneventful return journey, Josie arrived back to England which seemed grey and uninspiring. She did not feel settled. Stavros sent her a Christmas card, he had copied the verse from somewhere and signed his name. Josie decided to work to save up enough money to go back to Piraeus again. She registered with a bureau doing temporary work learning modern technology and trades as she moved around. Weekends she would go dancing with her friends but did not meet anybody special.

One night after getting home late, Josie made a drink, put her electric blanket on and sat at the table where her father had left his pools coupon spread on top of an open newspaper. A classified advert caught Josie's eye saying: "Girl seeks others for working holiday in Rome." Intrigued she made contact and met Sofia, a very small redhead with streaming long hair from

London. She wanted to go to Rome to work and needed company. Although Sofia had no work to go to nor address to stay, Josie was read to join her.

Sofia lived with her parents in a maisonette in North London. Josie slept on the floor in the living room. The next day Sofia, Josie and another girl called Rita who always wore black, caught a train to Rome. A fourth girl called Roberta joined them, she had a job at the Excelsior Hotel, Rome, because she spoke a few languages. The girls booked sleepers and were woken up for passports at the borders.

Before leaving England, Josie had a premonition that she would meet someone who appeared to know her. Something important would happen to change her life. The afternoon of arrival in Rome, Rita, Sofia and Josie left their luggage in the pensione and went in search of Via Veneto to see the Hotel Excelsior. As they were walking down Via Veneto, a handsome man stopped Josie asking if her name was Elizabet. He said he thought he knew her, asked where she was staying, kissed her hand then walked off with his two friends.

Early the following morning when they were all asleep, there was a knock on the bedroom door. Josie had a visitor. Slipping her coat over her nightdress, she was startled to find the handsome man waiting for her. Josie was so embarrassed, she wanted to disappear. He had called to invite the three girls to go sightseeing, he had a car waiting. The other two had to return to the Train station to collect some luggage. They sent Josie in advance and made a rendezvous for later.

The sightseeing tour was fun followed by lunch, so began Josie's romance with Giovanni Morano. He was tall, grey layered hairstyle, green eyes, tanned, oozed charm and sang love songs loudly in the street as he walked along. Sofia had a plastic doll which was pregnant on one side. The maid moved the doll onto Josie's bed, plastic side up. Josie was not amused, she was wooed, pursued and eventually seduced by Giovanni, who sent her romantic postcards when she went home. He gave her his silver name bracelet to wear.

To stay in Rome the girls needed to find work. They moved into a basement apartment near the university, with a tangerine tiled bathroom. Josie slept on a convertible sofa which said in Italian: "When you feel the urge to work, sit down here and wait for it to pass." Next door was a mature lady, Stella, who entertained gentlemen callers discreetly. Stella had lived an adventurous life in Latin America. Despite the language difficulties, they all became good friends.

One day the girls stopped for coffee and the guy making the coffee invited them to a club called SING SONG with his friends. They spent many happy evenings together. Josie met a sweet talking Libyan who promised her the world and took her to a fancy charity evening at the Hilton Hotel, which she didn't enjoy due to period pains. Giovanni remained Josie's only boyfriend. She didn't see him all the time as he lived in the suburbs.

The girls looked in the Rome Daily American newspaper for job vacancies. They were invited by an Italian lawyer who spoke no English, to work for him. As they struggled to communicate, he kept upping the salary. Josie found work for a travel agency located on Via Bissolati, typing itineraries for the Oberammergau Passion Play which featured that year. Every week Josie typed out an invoice saying, "Payment for translation services on the typewriter." The Italian office girls were unfriendly and unhelpful. They wilfully did not understand English. Josie remembered her school girl French and tried sticking an 'o' on the end of words.

When summer arrived, it became too hot in Rome. Josie found a job with an Italian family who were going to their holiday home in Marzocca, a resort near Ancona and Senigalia. The father was a banker from Rome. One of his daughters, Rita was arriving from Athens where her husband worked for IBM. She had two children. The other daughter, Carla, was a young widow with a small son called Carlo. Josie's role was to help the widow translate tourist information into good English, for a tourist guide examination she was taking, e.g. slabs of marble.

Josie had a small room just off the kitchen. After lunch when the family took a siesta, Josie was free. Sitting on the beach opposite the house one afternoon, she saw three UFOs in the sky. They looked like flying saucers all suspended at an angle. Josie looked around to show somebody, but it was deserted, and all was quiet in the house. After a few minutes hovering, the three craft shot off at a diagonal angle at high speed.

Senigalia was an old market town with a bustling market. Josie bought two sweaters and a smart midi skirt there. She got to know the locals. One afternoon Josie and the Banker sat watching a children's cartoon on TV together. The little boy lost interest and wandered away. Josie thought the bank colleagues would be surprised if they knew.

During the summer Rose came to Marzocca living with the family next door. Giovanni also went to see Josie. They returned to Rome only to find that Josie had to return home due to health issues at home. Being an only child, Josie felt obliged to go. Josie's mother was delicate, at various times Josie had managed to run the household from an early age. Aunty Betty was diagnosed with cancer so could not help. So, after an exciting Italian interlude Josie returned home.

A permanent job was offered to Josie at James Barnes paper merchants due to the forthcoming marriage of one of the girls. She would not be returning. There was a young staff and it was convenient. Josie made two lifelong friends working there, one was called Jill, the other was Samantha who temped all summer and won a free holiday to Spain because of it.

Samantha had a Dutch boyfriend, so Josie, Samantha and two friends went for a long weekend to Amsterdam, Rotterdam, the Haigh and stayed locally with the boyfriend. The Dutch liner was superb, the English ferry on the return journey was falling apart. Josie enjoyed the sightseeing and was amused by the similar stores and brands they found there. There was even a Dutch Salvation Army singing outside C&A. In the red light district, the girls saw chairs in windows but not the occupants. Bars advertised smoking cannabis. Bicycles abounded, the Dutch bulbs were colourful, it was clean and pleasant wherever they went.

Josie worked and saved to travel again. There were a group of girls who rang around at weekends. They would meet in town and go to the clubs, sometimes boyfriends would go along. It meant that nobody had to stay in alone. To save money, Josie shared a taxi with John Cooper Clarke, the poet, and his friends Mike and Dave. They shared gossip, best party locations, happenings. The DJ from the Twisted Wheel lived locally too.

Josie found a better job in the Town Hall City Engineer's office where she went day release to College. She was placed in a large typing pool. The desks were arranged in two central rows facing each other, with the supervisor at the front of the room. As Josie sat down on the first day, she inadvertently pushed the manual typewriter off the desk where it fell with a resounding crash. There was silence, the typewriter was expensively repaired, and Josie was warned to take more care.

Meanwhile, Rose and Vicky were doing A-levels, Lizzie was working for a lawyer, Samantha was temping. A new friend sitting opposite Josie called Val, joined the group with her best friend Aimee. The other girls in the typing pool were older, two newlyweds and one matronly spinster who went on holiday with her mother to Tunisia, came back having found a husband and left. Irene was a floating Town Hall temp and good fun, but she had a steady boyfriend so did not go out.

Manchester Town Hall, a large gothic building had many ornate nooks and crannies, external balconies, public rooms and a museum type ambience, stood in Albert Square facing a big monument to Queen Victoria. Josie counted the votes after one election to earn extra money. Weddings and functions took place at times. Filming Sherlock Holmes and other productions also happened with props being carried around like imitation lampposts with costumed actors walking around.

Sofia nicknamed Piccolina, was obsessed by everything Italian. She loved the music, the handsome men, the style, everything. Josie and Sofia travelled back to Rome on the train towards Christmas 1971. They stayed in a cheap pensione where the patrone brought a doll round to be kissed. On Christmas eve the patrone handed out a slice of Panettone.

Giovanni went around to see Josie. He seemed subdued and the atmosphere was strained between them. It seemed Giovanni had been seeing Monica, a girl from Prague, who had gone back. Josie felt uncertain as to whether she felt anything for him now. They went out to get to know each other again. Giovanni kept saying "one day" for everything. He was still good looking and personable but seemed to lack ambition. They got on well but may have parted company if Josie's period had not been late. She thought it may have been down to the change in water and diet.

When time moved along, Josie told Giovanni who immediately proposed marriage. He would arrange a quiet ceremony he said. The idea of abortion in a Catholic country, would not be considered. As a foreigner alone, Josie did not know what to do. Josie felt young and was not ready for marriage, let alone motherhood. Whilst Giovanni was good company, he was not ideal husband material. He worked intermittently, always appeared well dressed and groomed, but Josie felt uncertain. She felt foolish, careless and thought of the shame she would bring upon her family if she returned home pregnant.

The wedding ceremony was short and in Italian. Josie wore her best dress. She did not know the witnesses or understand much. Both sets of parents were informed after the event. Josie's mother was disappointed and warned Josie that marriage was for keeps, she could not give up when she was fed up. Josie asked about moving to Manchester. Her mother disapproved, said unemployment was rising there. They should give Rome a go first. Giovanni's parents were reserved and spoke no English. His sister Maria was only slightly more welcoming.

Giovanni worked more often and obtained an old inexpensive rented apartment for them in Fiano Romano. It was small and basic, but Josie tried to keep it clean and added a few homely touches. The first meal she made for Giovanni was sausage and mash. He asked her where the sauce was. Josie told him there was no sauce with this dish. Giovanni said his mother always made sauce with meals, her meal was too dry. They had their first dispute.

Josie found work in a legal firm, typing in English. She travelled to Rome daily. Her colleagues were different age groups and distant. Sofia had gone back to London, so she had no friends. Although Josie was slowly picking up Italian, she felt an outsider very much on family occasions. Giovanni asked his mother to teach Josie to cook, but she felt too hot, tired and bothered when she came home from work.

In her ninth month Josie had not gained much weight, a tourist tried to chat her up on the bus. In movies and books marriage was a bed of roses. Although Josie and Giovanni did not argue, they lived like an old married couple. The hand held walks in Villa Borghese stopped, the romantic love songs by Massimo Ranieri, were no longer sung to her. Sometimes Giovanni would disappear or come home late. Josie didn't mind, she enjoyed the space. Giovanni was always ready for sex, Josie was not used to the heat, they had no air conditioning, it was difficult.

Shopping was also proving to be difficult locally. In England supermarkets were starting to replace small shops. At first it was a novelty to select goods and put them into a trolley, without queuing to be served. In Rome Josie learned to buy milk from a café bar, salt from a hardware shop, she could point at food on markets, but needed her phrasebook to ask for things inside the old fashioned grocers. English was not widely spoken. Rome was hot and crowded, especially during the tourist season. Josie was finding life uncomfortable and difficult.

The neighbour on their landing knocked on and told Josie she needed to share the cleaning of the stairs and landing. Momentarily, Josie wondered why she was being told before realising that now she had responsibility. Giovanni did not do housework and expected his laundry to be kept clean, food to be available and tried to teach Josie to speak Italian. Josie did not feel grown up enough to cope, she wanted somebody to take care of her.

Aimee took two weeks leave to visit Josie to help her just before the baby was due. When Josie went into labour she turned to Aimee, who found Giovanni and went into the taxi with them to the hospital, holding Josie's hand. Giovanni and Aimee were sent home to wait. Josie was given an enema and left on the toilet for so long, she thought she would drop the baby there. She huffed, puffed and delivered a baby daughter in the middle of the night.

Giovanni was excited to see his little girl. They decided to give her an Italian name, Chiara Giulia after his grandmother. Their apartment was not suitable with a narrow staircase, only one bedroom and the kitchen was more basic than Grove Street had been. Josie struggled to feed the baby who never seemed satisfied and cried night and day. Resorting to bottles to the disapproval of the family, Josie decided they would go back to England. Josie wanted her daughter to speak English and be educated at home. Giovanni was willing to give it a try.

BACK IN MANCHESTER

The family adored Chiara and made room for Josie and Giovanni to stay in the family apartment. It was a bit crowded and awkward at mealtimes with two families sharing the kitchen. Josie cooked very differently from her mother who remained a traditional cook. They decided to enquire about staying. Council housing was not available, there was a long waiting list. If one of them had a permanent job, they could apply for a mortgage after six months and buy a house.

Chiara was a very active baby who didn't sleep much. She had to settle into a new routine and cried when she got bored or irritable. When she was outside or on the move, Chiara was happy. She looked like Giovanni with his green eyes, elfin face. People everywhere commented how pretty she was. Sometimes Giovanni had to take her for a walk outside in her pram to get her settled at night.

Giovanni took a job in a local chemical plant, but his English was not very good. He couldn't understand what was expected of him. He enrolled on a one year course at college to do the Cambridge English for Foreign Students examination which he passed. Giovanni made friends on the course and followed it up with an accounting course. After he finished studying, Giovanni was unable to get a job despite countless interviews. A Spanish chef offered him restaurant work and a butcher was willing to train him, but Giovanni did not want to do that kind of work.

Whilst studying Giovanni sometimes went out with the other students, a few trips were arranged. Josie was pleased he had made friends. They decided that Giovanni would take Chiara to a nursery and collect her daily, whilst Josie found a permanent job. She went for an interview at the prestigious Midland Hotel, where the rich and famous stayed when in Manchester. It had a plaque announcing it was where Mr Rolls met Mr Royce. Giovanni asked Josie why she was applying, he felt they would prefer somebody glamorous.

Josie was hired, she worked with a part time girl married to a Spanish man with two sons. Menus had to be typed and printed in English and French, daily plans of functions and activities, plus correspondence had to be answered. The French Chef was loud and temperamental. The Banqueting Manager was married to a Swedish girl, he was full of fun. Managers would place a wreath on the toilet door if anybody lingered too long. It was always busy and interesting, varying daily.

Once Josie's job became permanent and she had worked for six months, they began to look for a house of their own. Women were only recently allowed to apply for mortgages and do their own banking, it used to be only available to males. Some houses had dry rot or other hidden problems. They could not afford the best areas, but managed to find a terraced house with two bedrooms. It had the bathroom located off the main bedroom, two living rooms with a small fitted kitchen off the back. There was an outside toilet in the yard, plus another one in the bathroom. It was convenient for the nursery, school for later, there were local shops. Most of the neighbours were young marrieds. Josie used her life savings for the deposit and simple furnishings. The seller left a bar in the front room which pleased Giovanni, although it was not stocked.

All was going well until Josie found herself pregnant again. An aunt asked her why she was pregnant when Giovanni had not found a job. Josie was annoyed by the question. As an only child, Josie had always been responsible when her mother's health suffered, or family crises occurred, she did not want Chiara to be burdened. Although Josie had not planned the pregnancy, she thought it would be good to have a second child then stop. She did not want a big family.

Chiara was walking and into everything, trying to talk. She liked music and would totter about on her baby legs when her favourite tunes came on the radio. Josie had two willing babysitters, Aunty Betty on her mother's side and Aunty Sadie on her father's. Giovanni and Josie would go out on Saturdays, leaving Chiara with her grandparents. They went to markets, local towns, seaside, events for the day, have some lunch and return to collect Chiara at teatime.

Occasionally, Josie and Giovanni went out at night. They went to see Boney M in concert, the curtain behind their act was silver shimmering fabric. A group of friends went to a Drydock boat disco, dancing to all the hits. For a special birthday they went to Tiffany's in the town centre. Giovanni helped with the routines in the house and could often be seen pushing Chiara around. She seemed to enjoy the nursery and was full of energy until she dropped after bath time.

Meanwhile, Vicky had married and had a son. Rose had married and taken a teaching contract with her husband in New Zealand for two years. Aimee had gone travelling round the States with her friend Ruth. Samantha was working and travelling. Lizzie had married a policeman, had a son and was expecting her second child at a similar time to Josie. They arranged that Josie would have Lizzie's boy whilst she gave birth. When the time came they both had baby boys on the same day in different hospitals.

Josie's son was small and gentle, dark hair and a quiet personality. They called him Alessandro. Chiara was not very interested in him because he was not old enough to play. As he grew bigger and tried to copy Chiara, she bossed him about and often overwhelmed him. When Alessandro was only a few months old, Lizzie came visiting with her family who stayed overnight. The two babies were placed side by side. Lizzie's husband nearly took the wrong baby as Josie's mother had bought two identical outfits for presents.

Josie had to go to work early the next morning, so she tiptoed about quietly leaving everybody sleeping. She noticed the kitchen door was unlocked, frowning she locked the door and went to work. Later she discovered Lizzie's husband had gone to the outside toilet wearing just thin pants and a tee shirt on a frosty morning. He had been locked out and nobody heard him knocking. When she found out, Josie was mortified.

At Christmas Josie invited her parents and two aunts for a festive meal. They wore paper hats and watched the Queen afterwards. They also gathered together to watch the Eurovision Song Contest. Giovanni was a gracious host. Chiara was indulged and the centre of attention. Josie was always busy trying to keep up with work and home. They had a telephone and tried to keep in touch with both families sending photos to Rome. Josie's father had been sent to Naples in the war and had an Italian girlfriend, so he had a soft spot for the country. His ship had been torpedoed and he'd been transferred to Africa, so his romance had ended.

Josie felt like the man of the family, handling the paperwork, earning, running things. Giovanni was increasingly frustrated about being unemployed. He was good with the children, but the marriage began to decline. Family and friends all rallied to Giovanni's defence, it was not his fault he could not find work. Josie was told not to upset him more by destroying the family. Josie had a suspicion that Giovanni had been unfaithful to her with another student, he neither admitted nor denied the accusation. With his striking good looks, women fancied him wherever they went.

Giovanni received news of a job offer in Rome so to persevere with the marriage, they put the house up for sale. They left it in the hands of Simba, a solicitor from Zimbabwe who later became a High Court Judge there. The furniture and belongings were packed up and shipped over in a container, so they could start over comfortably. A rental apartment had been reserved in a new district near Rome, on the top floor with international neighbours. Josie hoped the new job would provide a fresh start to the marriage.

When they first moved to Rome they were busy setting up house. The children cried because they didn't understand the language. Giovanni's sister Maria was paid to look after the children because Josie needed to work full time. She found a job working for an Egyptian shipping company for a man she nicknamed Horrible Henry who got distraught when he could not find some papers. Henry started shouting and flapping, so Josie told him to calm down, it was only a piece of paper. Next thing Personnel asked Josie if she wanted a transfer. She left and heard that when her successor was ill one day, Horrible Henry rang her at home to ask where something was, not how she was.

The next job was for an Iranian Petrochemical Company. Josie's boss was a lovely South African man nicknamed Super Duper Cooper. He wanted to see an Italian wedding, so Giovanni took him to one. Two of his photos jammed in his camera so the happy couple came out getting married in the middle of the sea. The workforce was multinational with mixed age groups. The toilets were unisex. It was not the most exciting work, but steady. Josie made friends from work and arranged to go out occasionally to see a movie or for a drink after work.

Giovanni was not pleased that Josie wanted to socialise. He said she should go out with him. He said she should take the children, or he would get a babysitter, so he could go as well. He wanted to know what time she would be back. Josie felt trapped and annoyed. When Giovanni wanted to go out or do anything, he never consulted her. Josie felt entitled to have a bit of time out to feel like a person instead of only wife, mother, dogsbody.

The marriage was in trouble. Giovanni and Josie were not bad people, just mismatched. He became critical and negative towards Josie who felt her self esteem slipping. There was no harmony in the home. Josie thought one day that if she never saw her husband again, it would be ok. The thought shocked Josie deeply, it was the beginning of the end which took a harrowing 18 months to achieve. At first Giovanni moved back to his mother's but had access to the family apartment and came when he wanted, removing things at will including the children's presents. All the family came to see Josie to pressurise her into staying married, in Italy it was very difficult to divorce.

A Danish family moved next door, all blonde. At first Sven the husband lived there with the eldest son. His wife, a former dancer, followed on with the youngest son. Josie became friends with the family, they all spoke English. Eventually, the wife returned to Denmark with the boys. Sven stayed a while longer before moving to South Africa. He taught Josie how to make a milk loaf and said: "Why do you stay with this man, he treats you so bloody?" He offered to look for work in South Africa for Josie, but she could not leave the children.

Josie received a telephone call from Giovanni at work one day, saying she needed to return home as Chiara was not well. When Josie arrived, Giovanni went to the house, shouted at her, slapped her and threw her out. Josie called the police who came out but said they did not interfere in domestic affairs. The apartment was in both names, so they could not throw one person out. Josie returned, and Giovanni left telling the policeman his tale of woe in rapid Italian.

Giovanni then took all Josie's clothes away leaving just the clothes she was wearing. Friends, neighbours and work colleagues rallied round and brought their clothing to share. As Josie was still slim, she managed. She did not get her clothes back for a year when they were returned in black bin liners, crumpled and musty having been hidden somewhere. Sometimes she returned home to find unexplained messes or more things missing. Josie felt traumatised.

Josie consulted an English speaking legal aid group who specialised in helping women. The lady lawyer agreed to start divorce proceedings. Josie was advised on what to say, how to respond to questions. Giovanni took out a legal document preventing Josie from leaving Rome for one year, she could not use her passport. The lawyer told Josie to hang tight. A divorce court hearing was set up in regarding custody of the children. There was a panel of stern looking family court judges who asked Josie if she wanted to reconcile or divorce. Josie said she wanted to divorce.

Giovanni told the court that Josie was a loose woman with no morals, not fit to raise the children. One of the judges asked Giovanni to provide evidence, he couldn't. The judge asked Giovanni who would take care of the children. Giovanni said his mother would. The judge responded saying that with due respect, his mother had done her share. Children so young needed to be with their mother.

Josie had to say why she wanted the divorce. She cited cultural differences and lack of harmony in the home. Josie agreed to part with various household appliances for Giovanni. He was supposed to pay maintenance but never did. The divorce was granted. Josie felt exhausted and defeated. Giovanni and Josie walked away from the court without speaking, there was no sense of victory.

Life was busy for Josie, working all week, running the household. At weekends the children went to stay with their grandma. It was hard to feed, clothe and manage everything on one wage. Josie obtained advances each month on her pay. People struggled with overdrafts. Giovanni did not contribute or make much contact. Friends told Josie about a job in a Bank putting through international payments in English. It came up due to maternity leave. Josie was successful and enjoyed it, the money was slightly more but prices were constantly rising.

Rome frequently had strikes and protest marches. People would blow whistles, bang on objects and flourish banners. Josie would see them through the window at work. Lunchtimes she went around Upim and the local shopping centres. To save money, Josie made her own lunch and rarely went out or bought anything for herself. The children were her priority. Chiara went to nursery school and Alessandro was in nursery, but she still had fees to pay.

Eventually, a young girl from Croatia attached herself to Giovanni and they started dating. After some time, the girl's brother approached Giovanni telling him that in their country, men dated women they wanted to marry. He should either marry or leave his sister alone. Giovanni asked Josie what he should do. Josie advised Giovanni to make a new life for himself, to study or travel or do something. He should not tie himself down again so soon.

Upon receiving a wedding invitation from Giovanni and his new bride, Josie decided that as soon as the year ended, she would return to Manchester with the children who were on her passport. A good time to leave would be when Giovanni was on his honeymoon. She would not ask his permission and planned to hide the passports when she arrived in England. Giovanni wanted the children to attend his wedding, so they stayed over at grandma's. Josie refused to go, she did not want to be Wife no. 1 and Wife no. 2.

Alessandro's passport was close to expiring, now he was five years old he needed a passport of his own. Josie worried she may have a problem. She booked a flight and hoped for the best. Giovanni rang Josie at work from time to time. Josie told the receptionist at work to say she was on a course if he rang. One of the neighbours hid their luggage in her car boot and offered to drive them to the centre airport bus. They could leave home as if they were going shopping. The neighbour would hand in the keys in an envelope a week afterwards. If Giovanni called round, the neighbour would say the family had gone out.

Josie always spoke to the children in English. When she had time, she gave them English lessons using her old school book The New First Aid in English. Chiara was very bright, she always got a good report. Alessandro seemed to be enjoying h nursery. After telling the children they were going on a trip, Josi told them not to say anything at school. Alessandro left his clas saying goodbye, he's going to England.

They left their apartment wearing unseasonably warm clothes due to a late heatwave, as if they were going shopping. The flight was delayed overnight so Josie found a friend who lived i Rome, who agreed to let them stay over. When they arrived at Fiumicino Airport the flight to Manchester had been delayed a further couple of hours to allow a London flight to take priority. Josie felt agitated. Until the flight departed, Josie could not relax. They arrived to a snowy scene. Josie's father was waitir to meet them. They took a bus into the city; the driver was covered in snowflakes each time he went out to get luggage. The kids thought it was very amusing.

At Josie's parents her old bedroom was kitted out with two single beds for the children. Josie had to sleep on a small two seater sofa in the living room. During the night her parents would get up to go to the toilet or make a drink. The doors banged, and the living room was never dark due to windows fitted along the hallway and from the balcony. It was hard to sleep and not comfortable. Josie's neighbour in Rome rang to say Giovanni had been round and sent the police to find them. She advised hiding the passports in a bank.

The children were enrolled in school, Chiara was in the first year of the high school, Alessandro joined the juniors. Chiara was always competitive and liked to be the best. After her first low marks, she worked hard and became top of the class ever after. Eventually Chiara became head girl. Alessandro won a prize for advancing three years in his English studies. He worked at a steady pace and was not competitive. Both made friends quickly. Josie could not afford to indulge them with all the latest things other children took for granted.

Josie went to the Housing Department to be added on the list. They gave her low points. At the time children were not supposed to live in multi storey buildings, so Josie had an interview with the Housing Officer and explained her predicament. The fact that Josie had a permanent job to go to in a Government office was also helpful. It was very difficult to get any rest on the little sofa, Josie explained. Eventually, she was offered a three bedroomed central heated semi with a garage near Heaton Park. Josie accepted so fast, she moved in the moment she received the keys.

Brentford Nylons had a big store on the corner of Piccadilly, it was closing down so Josie bought beds, a cooker, fridge and washing machine in the sale. Argos equipped her with a table and chairs, a cheap 3 piece suite, dishes and pans. Josie had posted ahead towels and linens in cardboard boxes which arrived safely. Everything was basic, but it was private and peaceful with a good circular bus service.

Manchester had its share of Quango organisations at the time including: Equal Opportunities, The Commission for Racial Equality, others related to environmental issues and local Government operations. Josie found a long term placement working with another girl flat out, trying to deal with all the correspondence and queries. The office structure was a mini United Nations. The job lasted for over a year until funds were cut, so Josie registered with an agency while she tried to find a permanent role.

Changes had occurred in England whilst the family had been away including American fast food chains, new push button telephones, explicit sex programmes and page 3 girls. Punk styles were in vogue. Alessandro saw his first punk on the bus, squeezed Josie's hand and said loudly: "Look mummy, an Indian." He also asked loudly on a quiet bus "Is that a boy or a girl?" Chiara asked a lady in the bus queue what colour pyjama she wore. The queue waited for the lady's response which was pink one week, lilac the next!

Chiara was in the high school choir which took part in an international competition, the final was to be held in Rome. The school reached the finals stage, so Josie thought it would be a good idea for Alessandro to go too, to visit their grandparents. She knew she was taking a risk. Over the years Josie had made peace with Giovanni who had started a new family. He rarely kept in touch with Chiara and Alessandro, but Josie knew he would be pleased to see them. She telephoned and arranged for Alessandro to be met at the airport and explained about the competition which would be televised. An air hostess would look after Alessandro both journeys.

Whilst the children were away, Josie took the opportunity to accompany Sofia to an alternative holiday in Spain for a week. She could not afford it but manipulated her purse strings and paid herself back for months afterwards. The Cortijo was a vegetarian retreat with holistic therapies, walks, trips, swimming pool with the accommodation surrounding it. Josie was the only passenger from Manchester. Most of the group attending flew from London.

Josie was met at the airport, Sofia was there before her. From Malaga airport Josie transferred into the Sierra Nevada mountains to a small village about an hour outside Granada. Sofia and Josie shared a twin bedded room with en suite bathroom. Outside there was a pond with frogs croaking all night. On the roof was one bedroom inadvertently given to the only guest who was disabled and couldn't manage the stairs. There was a meditation room, optional outings and activities were offered. The group went on walks, picnics, had a day out visiting Alahambra Palace in Granada.

Although it was May, it was hot compared to England. Locals were still wearing their winter clothes. The tourists were in shorts and tee-shirts. Meal times were taken on a patio, buffet style. Sofia and Josie teamed up with a couple linked to the Green Party, and a single man called James from Wales, who had a brother living in the Manchester area. All the food was freshly grown and prepared, the homemade bread was delicious. Next door was a bar where guests served themselves and left money in the honesty box. The scenery was picturesque with mountain views and little white washed Andalucian villages tucked away.

The group were of mixed nationalities all friendly. An American man related how he had accidentally knocked a display of toys over in a major London store. When he asked if he could help to pick everything up, the assistant told him frostily he had done enough. One couple had met through a dating advertisement, but their romance didn't last. A lady was so enamoured with the area, she bought an old house in the mountains to renovate. It was a week of fun in picturesque surroundings. At the end of the holiday everybody spent a day at the seaside before leaving for the airport. Only the Manchester flight was delayed.

The children returned from Rome happy to be home. Chiara's choir did not win the competition. Both children said they had enjoyed their holiday. They did not talk about Giovanni and his family much, but seem to have had a pleasant visit. In the way of children, they settled down and carried on with their normal routines. They did not ask to go again and did not return to Rome for years. Occasionally, Giovanni wrote. Josie encouraged the children to send him birthday cards and never badmouthed him. He was their father.

James was married, his wife had been doing exams during the holiday which is why he was alone. When he visited his brother in Cheshire, he paid a visit to show Josie the holidays photos, staying overnight. He came loaded up with delicious goodies. The children discovered some fancy breakfast cereal in the cupboard and polished it off. When James opened the packet for his breakfast, it was empty. Josie had to instruct them to keep their hands off. For a time, Josie kept in touch with the Green Party couple, plus Sofia and James but life was too busy

Josie had taken driving lessons as a teenager but after an incident when the car engine overheated and exploded, she had been put off and abandoned the lessons. With deregulation of public transport, Josie realised that she needed to learn to drive. Her father was not well, he had a stroke and was sent to convalesce in a home off the local bus route. Josie needed to collect her mother to visit the home regularly. It took Josie two attempts to pass the driving test, the first time the inspectors called out her name, Josie's nerves took over. The second time she took some calming tablets and managed it. She bought a second hand Metro car from the garage down the road.

Chiara was taking her GCEs. When the results were due, the whole family were on a budget holiday in Northumberland. Rather than wait, Chiara took the train back to Manchester to collect her 8 x A grades and 1 x B grade results. She decided to stay on at school to do her Advanced GCEs choosing biology, chemistry, maths and general studies. Josie was very proud of her and grateful that Chiara did not need any assistance with her homework. Alessandro was an average pupil, neither top nor bottom, good at subjects he enjoyed like his mother. He was not studious, preferred music and films. His room had decks and cases of records.

Chiara took a computing course and obtained another A grade. Alessandro also had a flair for computing. Josie bought a simple computer which came in useful for all the family to use. The children played computer games, Josie kept her correspondence and social affairs in order on it. New advanced developments were constantly upgrading appliances, televisions, computers. Records were replaced by cassettes and vinyl discs. Video shops sprung up offering a selection of films to watch at home, so many cinemas closed. Microwaves viewed at first with suspicion became part of the kitchens everywhere.

To pay for driving lessons, Chiara got a weekend job at Sainsbury where she worked part time all her student years. When Alessandro was old enough, he got a similar part time job at Tesco, riding his bike to and fro. Both children worked hard and saved to buy themselves music centres, games, fashions, it taught them the value of money. All the family made sandwiches together in the evenings, had a rota for washing up. and shared cleaning the house once a week. The family motto was "anybody who cannot clean their house once a week, does not deserve to have one."

Josie joined two rambling groups, one mid week and one at weekend. She went to keep fit classes at work, swimming with Vicky sometimes and contacted her friends. Rose was married with a daughter, living in New Zealand teaching. Aimee had a son and was working in legal aid. Lizzie had three children and was working full time at a university. Samantha had been engaged to be married, was looking for houses to buy, found herself pregnant when her fiancé disappeared never to be seen again. With help from her family, Samantha was raising her son and working for a national newspaper. Eleanor, a former school friend who used to sit in front of Josie, was still single so they paired up and went gallivanting.

Josie tried a few singles events. Women far outnumbered the men who were surrounded. Josie did not feel comfortable and was not sure she wanted to meet anybody, she thought it would be good to have a male friend to hang out with. Eleanor met somebody at a civic hall 60s night dance. Josie found a single man friend who took her out for a drive each Sunday afternoon when they tried to put the world to rights, but no romance. Being single and independent gave Josie freedom of choice in her life, she found it satisfying and did not feel inclined to pander to a man's will or take care of one.

After a party one night a guy chattered up Josie saying she had his favourite hairstyle. They chatted, and he took her home. When Josie asked if he would like a coffee, he entered the house and pounced on her, wandering hands, breathless, he went out quicker than he entered. Another time she met a personable man at a talk, they had seemed to have common interests. The problem was that he lived in Jersey, had been over visiting. They managed to communicate for a time and visited each other, but distance won out and they lost contact.

Josie and her friends often spoke about putting the world to rights, so when opportunities came along they took them. Lizzie and Josie went on a Catholic Retreat to listen to Father Angelo de Mello who was a charismatic spiritual speaker. The theme was "Awareness" which gave them insights into universal issues. They both bought one of his books and tried to live up to his standards, but real life intervened making them crash down to earth.

Next came an Encounter weekend at the University on the theme of Judaism Faces Modernity. Aimee, Lizzie and Josie went along to listen to Rabbi Abraham Twerski, a prolific author, psychiatrist and founder of a rehab centre in America for substance abuse. His audiences were so large, an overflow with a screen had to be set up. A quietly spoken man who never repeated his punch lines, Rabbi Twerski resembled Rip Van Winkle with his white beard, but was so inspirational, Lizzie bought several books of his and was a lifelong fan. Josie was so inspired after listening to him, she thought about religion for the first time. Aimee bought a couple of his books.

Next came a 'More to Life Retreat' in Shropshire where Eleanor and Josie spent a weekend in a stately home with grounds playing games, listening to lectures and enjoying themselves. Everybody brought along their favourite book and had to explain why. On the Saturday evening there was a session of courtly ballroom dancing. Josie accidentally found herself leading a line of women around the room, joining up with the teacher leading the men. Nobody knew exactly how to do the routine, but the giggles made it all worthwhile.

When the Dalai Lama came to Manchester, all the girls went to see him. He made Josie and Lizzie shed a tear. In a busy stadium, some people wandered around whilst the Dalai Lama was speaking. Josie thought it was very disrespectful. As a speaker, the Dalai Lama was modest and often laughed at himself. Realising how much suffering he must have seen and faced, the struggles over the years in exile, Josie became a lifelong fan. He spoke sense and told this audience there was no need to become a Buddhist, everybody could learn from their own religion.

During a pub quiz Josie realised how many great musicians had died including Elvis, Buddy Holly, John Lennon, Dusty Springfield, Roy Orbison, T-Rex. Music and fashions had changed a great deal. There had been Flower Power with hippies, dope, men with long hair, the Beatles seeking transcendental meditation in India. The older generation disapproved and asked men if they were girls to be provocative. Along came the Thatcher era and Dynasty tv show with the padded shoulders and business suits. Women wanted equal rights, men in general earned more to perform the same roles.

Punks came along with hairstyles like Indian head feathers. They were followed by goths with dark makeup and pale faces.

Old styles were revived, new styles included ripped jeans around the legs. Brands were worn as labels outside the clothes to show their status. It became a throwaway society, being cheaper to replace shoes than repair them. Credit was extended and offered to all, things could be obtained on impulse with payment in instalments. Savings dwindled when instant gratification was applied.

Josie had a boyfriend, Isaac who she met on business. He had never been married, had a musical background and worked in antiques. For a time, they were happy, he constantly challenged Josie to open her mind, broaden her horizons. She met his family and they attended community functions and concerts together. The children were uncertain about him but were busy in their own lives. If Josie was happy, they didn't mind. Isaac became controlling, he wanted to know all Josie's movements, he wanted to borrow her car and use it to collect her, he rang the house at unexpected times. Josie felt stifled and irritated. Exit Isaac after a blazing row.

Chiara was graduating, Josie went with her mother to the ceremony, feeling very proud. She had entered the Milk Round applying to all the major employers for work. Competition was rife, and Chiara found it hard to get a place. Her first role was in London where she shared a house in the suburbs. She worked for a charity promoting events and selling raffle tickets. This meant working unsociable hours and often having to store raffle prizes. With the advent of mobile phones Chiara was constantly on call. There was even a fax telephone in the house printing out instructions.

Josie had arranged for her parents to move to Sheltered Accommodation as they grew older. Upon arrival her mother met a former school friend and said, "Clara, you haven't changed a bit." Josie saw Clara as a little old lady, permed grey hair and glasses. Two of her mother's friends used to visit for afternoon tea and gossip once a week. Her mother always said, "the girls are coming" even though they were all pensioners. Josie's father used to help all the neighbours doing odd jobs even though he was not particularly talented. He would talk to people in the street, everywhere he went.

Josie's father developed dementia, the onslaught took time until he had to go into a home because he had a habit of wandering off. Josie's mum could not lift him or cope, she was much smaller than him. Every weekend the family would go to visit Josie's dad taking some delicacies to eat. He was subdued in the home, there was a broken television in his room. Frequently he asked to go home.

Other times he was aggressive and rude. Towards his demise they were not certain he knew them. It was a very distressing time. Josie supported her mother at the funeral. Neighbours and family visited offering their sympathy. Josie tried to take her mother out for a drive at weekends. Increasingly, her mother grew tired and reluctant to do much. One day when Josie rang her mother's purse had been snatched from her hand whilst out shopping. Josie was furious but could not do anything.

Her mother needed regular blood checks at the hospital. On a routine visit her mother was knocked over, broke her hip, had emergency surgery leading to a heart attack, then died. Eleanor had been visiting Josie's mother at the time so rallied round and rang to inform everybody. Josie found herself an orphan. She had to decorate and empty her parent's apartment. Chiara helped and ruthlessly threw away anything that was not used. was a difficult with sentimental value detracting from the task.

Alessandro had stayed working at the supermarket whilst he studied part time. Instead of university, he did everything the hard way. He had a flair for computer technology, but his interests remained music and film. Sometimes Alessandro did DJ gigs. Alessandro had a good social life with his friends, but still lived with Josie. They lived harmoniously, although Josie always felt protective of him. With work and studies, Alessandro did not have much free time but still managed to go on holiday to Austria climbing mountains.

Chiara found a better job in Sales and Marketing. She wanted to find a job nearer home but live independently. Her boyfriend Ben came from Cheshire. As a financial advisor, he travelled about and was based in London temporarily. A lucrative offer propelled him back to Cheshire where he invited Chiara to join him. Ben was an intelligent, focused on his future career plan. His family welcomed Chiara and told Josie it would be better to see how they managed together as a couple before making any commitment.

Ben's brother offered Chiara a role in the IT company he ran with friends. She accepted and helped to grow the business. They bought a small modern house on the South side of Manchester and got engaged. At their engagement party were family friends and relations amongst them was former neighbours, the Jones who brought along one of their daughter's Elise who was home from university. Alessandro and Elise were introduced several times which amused them. They went for a drink, made a few dates which eventually turned into their own engagement.

Alessandro had obtained qualifications and moved up the job ladder until he was an IT manager, supervising trainees. He took Elise to a fancy restaurant to propose. With their combined income they were able to buy a small modern house in a good area. Her parents and Josie were good friends. Ben's family were also very welcoming. Chiara and Elise became best friends. Chiara was bridesmaid for Elise.

Josie managed to make a few home improvements once the house was empty. She had an inexpensive new kitchen, changed some of the doors, decorated and upgraded her car which had aged and needed money spending on it. She worked full time at a high spec computer company. Josie had a PA/Admin role which kept her busy. She was a good organiser and there was always pressure. Conditions of employment were modern and pleasant with perks. There was free fresh fruit, free toiletries, keep fit sessions with a mini gym, plus discounts in some stores.

Three times Josie had been made redundant. The first time she locked herself in the toilets and cried. How would she manage to support her family? What would she do? She registered with several agencies and did temporary work, constantly applying for jobs. The second time she had a good job with the Co-op HQ, but it downsized, and her role vanished. Updating her skills at each assignment, Josie temped again until she got back into local Government. Due to budget cuts, she was surplus again.

The computer firm was fortunate because she had gone to the interview looking smart. When a storm erupted en route, Josie arrived like a drowned rat. Thanks to Alessandro who was a whizz computer kid, she was familiar with the terminology and trends. Although Josie worried she may not be able to keep up she did not have to. Her task was to take care of all the high flyers who could. It paid well, and Josie hoped to be able to stay put. Nobody felt secure in their work. Jobs for life had gone. Anybody who stayed in one job too long was viewed as lacking ambition. Josie was pleased she was not just starting out as competition for places was massive. Often applicants were ignored, only hearing if eligible for interview.

Josie kept in touch with her friends although they did not manage to meet up as often. All the children had grown up, most of her friends were married. Thankfully there were no druggies or scandals, everyone was busy trying to earn a buck and make a good life. Celebrations and special occasions were shared. Outings changed from nightclubs to day trips.

Giovanni and his son Phillipo came over for Chiara's wedding to Ben. He wanted to give her away. They stayed with Josie who felt pleased to see them but ambivalent about the reunion. Phillipo was a pleasant, innocent little boy, no trouble. He shared a room with his dad. During the days they stayed, Giovanni took Ben out visiting friends, exploring, whilst Josie worked. Chiara and Alessandro entertained them too. It was a pleasant visit, Giovanni rented the appropriate evening dress and a mini version for Phillipo.

Chiara was a glowing beautiful bride in a designer gown, Giovanni proudly led her into the hall where the wedding took place. Josie shed a few tears. The meal was tasty, the speeches witty and the music lively. It was a perfect wedding. Later everybody waved goodbye to the newlyweds who were staying in a city hotel overnight before leaving for their honeymoon in the Bahamas, leaving behind snowy cold Manchester. Giovanni also left, and Josie was surprisingly tearful waving him goodbye. She did not want him to stay, but she cried for what could have been.

In Autumn 1995 Josie went on an alternative holiday to Turkey with Eleanor, joining a small group. A Manchester girl married to a Turkish man took the group touring behind the tourist trails.

Based in Kas, it was authentic Turkish living with old villages and mosques. The blue skies, sea, pine clad slopes, calls to prayer, everything felt Middle Eastern. Various trips and outings were arranged including a trip to a Turkish bath for a massage. It was alarming to hear the slaps and pummelling behind the scenes, exhausting to have the treatment, then cosseted in towelling dressing gowns drinking apple tea.

Among the sites they visited was a Peace Village where Greek citizens were forcibly removed one night, leaving their homes and belongings to become a Ghost town. A similar move was made on the Greek shores. Until then both communities had lived and worked together. There was a Greek island offshore from Kas where Turkish residents were not allowed. The group hired a yacht for a day trip, raising a Greek flag. The Greek island was scenic but lacked the ambience of Kas.

Another time they stayed overnight at Mount Olympus where they climbed the mountain at dusk to see constant fires flaring up from holes in the mountain. There had been fires there for over 2,000 years. They saw Roman and Greek amphitheatres, had tea at a traditional Turkish tea house with a huge brass kettle hanging above a fire. A wedding procession passed by them with a goat wearing a red ribbon tied around its horns. On the mountain top inhabited only by isolated Bedouin, there was a glacial green freshwater lake and breathtaking scenery.

Shops and banks were open until midnight. It felt safe to walk about day and night. Women wore traditional dress. Many of th Kurdish men had pony tails and good bone structure. Leather and carpet shops welcomed visitors with endless cups of appl tea. There was a timeless air about Kas, space, light and a special atmosphere. Herbal teas were available everywhere used for cures, tonics and various purposes.

Back home Josie found a new boyfriend called Ian, they met when she volunteered to help serve refreshments at a local charity event. They conversed whilst events took place and discovered they had common interests. Without having met before, they seemed to know many of the same people. Ian looked up Josie's telephone number and called her to invite her out for a drink. Surprised and nervous, Josie rang Chiara and Elise to ask what to wear on a date. Alessandro was wary, he said that Josie should not just go off with an unknown man, so came around. Ian came to pick Josie up and was introduced to Alessandro before they went out.

After their first date there was silence for a while and no romance. Ian was divorced with grown children but had lost contact with them. His ex-wife had acquired the family home and the divorce had not been acrimonious, so Ian remained cynical and detached. As friends they went out at weekends sometimes, took a few holidays together. Ian was very set in his ways, as a successful businessman, he was sophisticated and self-assured. He was always on top of situations and had concealed supplies to suit every eventuality.

Josie enjoyed Ian's company, he made her laugh. He was interesting and intelligent, always one step ahead of her. There was no romance for a long time, both were cautious, Josie was disappointed. When she tried to make a move, Ian rejected her, so she felt mortified. In other ways Ian was considerate and constant. He would wait until she entered her house before driving off or accompany her and wait when she needed to go places. Apart from some hypochondria issues, Ian was fun.

Alessandro and Elise bought a small house on a modern estate then got married, it was a lively happy wedding. Ian sat next to Josie on the top table looking very debonair in his dinner suit.

Josie felt proud and happy to be seen with him. Often on special occasions, Josie felt noticeably single, she had nobody to smooch with.

Living alone seemed to suit Josie, she could please herself in every way. Having somebody else to please or cater to, seemed to be an unnecessary burden. She could watch the tv programmes she liked, eat simple food, get involved or detached from domesticity and it seemed ideal. Josie was modern without being trendy, active without being super fit, and tried to keep up to date with world affairs. As she had given up looking for a mate, she was surprised to have attracted Ian.

Ian wanted to move abroad either to Gibraltar where he had connections, or India where he felt there were up and coming trends. He wanted Josie to accompany him. Josie had lived abroad and was not drawn to either country. Josie felt inclined to go for a holiday perhaps, but was not ready to leave her family behind. She had managed to buy her home on the Council House Sales scheme and had furnished it debt free, so felt secure. As Chiara was pregnant, Josie had future grandchildren to think of. Ian wanted an answer.

Josie felt reluctant to move again but offered Ian a place to sta while he sold his house and arranged his affairs. Ian moved in with Josie. During the honeymoon period they managed considerately. Ian had the spare bedroom, he prepared his ow food mostly because he turned out to be a fussy eater. He alsc had set habits and aversion to mess, noise and other minor issues. As time progressed, Josie felt uncomfortable in her ow home. Ian became furtive, shutting himself away in his room, not communicating much, becoming sarcastic and scathing. T house was full of tension.

The evening before Ian left, he told Josie he would be departing the next day. He left belongings in his room which he said somebody would collect. Josie got up early the next morning to wave him off in the taxi. When Josie entered the spare bedroom, she was shocked and horrified to find the dusty cluttered mess. It was a tip. With the help of a friend, Josie laboured hard to clear the room. Although she was prepared to store Ian's belongings, her family were so annoyed with his behaviour, they took everything to the tip. Ian left no forwarding address and did not get in touch.

When Chiara gave birth to Olivia, Josie fell in love at first sight. It was as if Olivia was the first baby she had ever seen. From birth Josie adored Olivia and could not see enough of her. Elise and Josie went to the hospital carrying a balloon and teddy. Elise became pregnant shortly after giving birth to a handsome boy they called Josh. At the end of the following year both girls were pregnant again and gave birth within a fortnight of each other Chiara had Mark and Elise had Zak. Josie loved them all and became a regular babysitter. Josie became a typical over indulgent grandma.

All Josie's friends became grandparents too, although all felt too young for the stereotype role. It was fun to share exploits and photos of all the children. It seemed familiar to get involved in nursery then school events, helping with provisions and later homework. The four children went to the same school. Josie played games with them, tried to be strict but usually spoilt them because she didn't see them often enough to ever get fed up of them. They were so trusting and affectionate, Josie melted at their innocence.

It occurred to Josie that she was old enough to do anything she wanted within reason. She formed a topical discussion group in a Church Hall for over forties with refreshments. Sometimes there was a guest speaker. It was so successful, the caretaker had to flick the lights at the end to get people to leave. Some people were lonely, and the group was the only time they had to socialise all week. A few romances started resulting in one happy marriage. When Ian came along, he disapproved of Josie's involvement, so she quit. After he left, Josie felt too disheartened to start again. She just wanted space and peace.

The computer company Josie worked for was taken over and to save money, moved away long distance. Once again Josie had to job hunt. Through connections, Josie found a local job giving advice to customers on Government benefits and queries. It involved keeping up to date with ever changing legislature, endless repetition and trying to be pleasant. Josie cut her hours down to three days a week. She did not enjoy the role. She had always disliked cramming information that did not interest her. Although Josie began the role without prejudice, she found herself becoming very prejudiced with callers that expected everything for nothing.

When Josie made her final mortgage payment, she checked out her pension schemes and tried to evaluate when she could retire. If she worked an additional year, she would be entitled to about £89 extra. Taking the opportunity, Josie handed in her notice. A surprise party with a DJ was set up in the meeting room, with decorations, the whole company brought food to make a buffet. Josie was presented with gifts, a cheque, flowers, leaving on a high. Josie felt ecstatic.

With her retirement lump sum, Josie bought a new car and carried out some home improvements. The remainder was set to pay her a monthly sum which enabled her to live comfortably afford the annual holiday and pay her way. She lived modestly and with no mortgage or car payments, managed well. It seemed that Josie's pension was similar to her wage after deductions and major payments. With time to please herself, Josie researched how to spend her time.

It was a good era to retire, there were activities to suit everybody. Somebody's mother was making soft furnishings, there was art, rambling, volunteering, woodwork, maintenance, rambles, outings, lunch clubs. The list was endless, volunteering also offered a diverse range of activities locally. Josie opted for Zumba and helping at a homeless shelter. In between she went swimming with Vicky and picked the kids up from school once a week. There were talks to go to, aerobics, meetings, musical events. Josie's life was busy, something to do every day and she had never been happier. She did not miss work at all.

Josie felt that old age was something that affected other people. Inside she felt eternally young. She noticed changes to other people but was always surprised by changes to herself. Josie thought that our bodies kept us mobile for our lifespans, so if parts suffered from wear and tear, she felt annoyed and frustrated. Josie was not ready for old age so planned to keep active. She wrote a list of discoveries to the newspaper labelled:

Things people don't tell us about old age symptoms:
- age spots appear as brown blots on even the most flawless complexions
- a tendency to nod off whilst seated
- a need to write lists of what we are meant to do or remember
- a realisation we cannot do as much as we used to
- we cannot digest all types of food successfully
- if we don't do exercise we stay out of shape permanently

- sometimes we need to go to spend a penny more often
- we can't always remember names or where we know people from
- we don't relate to latest trends or fashions
- we take longer to adjust to new technologies
- we don't like to be rushed
- sometimes we feel intimidated by the speed of modern life

The Good Bits

- We don't have to impress anybody
- We are older and wiser than we have ever been
- We get concessions on travel, cinema, deals
- We don't have to keep up to date with anything
- We have been there and bought the tee shirt so are not easily impressed
- We can organise our lives to suit ourselves
- We are useful aids with grandchildren or family advisors if applicable
- We can say "what do you expect at this age?"
- There are more opportunities for fun and new adventures than ever before
- It's not too late to enjoy our time for ourselves instead of pleasing others

On the social scene Josie realised she had become invisible in most cases, but still managed to attract a younger male friend and had the occasional date.
It seemed to be strictly platonic, but Josie was comfortable with that.

Retirement

Years ago, retirement meant the gap between finishing work and waiting to die. These days the freedom of choice was limited only by the individual's desire. There was something for everyone to enjoy and participate in. Groups, organisations, societies, volunteering, even part time jobs offered time enhancing activities for all. We just needed to check out notice boards and advertisements in our local area and go for the most appealing. We could try new things or experiment with the familiar and best of all, were under no obligation. If we didn't like something, we didn't go again.

If we wanted to remain fit, we needed to remain active and watch our diet. The old saying of "use it or lose it" applied. We stiffen up easily if we don't take regular action. If we eat too much and don't burn some of it off by being active, it will stay put and we became fat and ungainly. Old age led to blood pressure, cholesterol and other symptoms. By maintaining healthy eating, it was possible to get these lowered. Vegetarianism or even Vegan lifestyles combined with regular exercise tended to do the trick. It didn't matter what exercise, just a brisk walk daily helped.

The aim was not to be too sedentary, house-car-eat-sit-sleep was not a format to enhance a person. We didn't need to be too self- indulgent, just because we loved cream cakes did not mean we needed to resemble one in human form. Chocolate was good but so was fresh fruit or even dried fruit for nibbles. Water cleansed the body much better than pop or sweet drink cans. The fruit and veg sections in the big supermarkets offered amazing year round varieties of fruits that we were only able to enjoy seasonally in days gone by.

Most of the time we snacked from habit or boredom. If we had three filling wholesome meals a day, it should be enough. Did we have enough interest in our lifestyle to keep us occupied? Just because we were older does not mean that we couldn't have fun or even romance. We may not be looking for lifetime mates, nor starting new families, but strange as it may seem, we are alive and ticking. Websites offer dating opportunities. We could make new friends doing our activities.

Once we became regulars at something, we were comfortable and enlarged our circle. There were walking groups, painting, sports, crafts, gardening, animals, school assistants, etc. no limits. Life could be more rewarding without the pressures of earning a living, raising a family or with a mortgage to pay. Hopefully, we could be able to live a more simple, modest lifestyle.

The best part of retirement was the freedom to choose how we spent our time. No more rush hour queues, deadlines, getting up before we are ready, unless we chose. If we didn't feel well, we were not obliged to go out to earn a living, we could rest if we wanted to. Our time was precious, so we did not need to waste it on activities that did not appeal to us. This was a beautiful powerful feeling. For years we have raced against the clock to meet our commitments and our obligations. Now we could watch others strive to do the same or even to get started on the rat race.

Some people go off on adventures to explore other countries seeking an alternative way of life. Some took up new hobbies activities. Others got fat and lethargic, often suffering from diabetes or high cholesterol. Over fifties were encouraged by the medical profession to take lifelong blood pressure and stat tablets. There was a sensation that life was speeding up and passing by much faster than before. Weeks flew by and we couldn't remember how we spent them. Information inundated us with fads and trends constantly changing. Certain foods are good for us one week and forbidden the next. There was a lack of continuity, nothing remained constant.

Josie ended her article there and sent it to the Evening News where she was published and enjoyed mini acclaim for a short time. All her new acquaintances agreed with her, several followed up on the joys of growing older. People with health issues refuted her claims. The majority were all in favour of retirement if in good health to be able to enjoy it. Clothing styles tended to be suitable for all ages, long gone were the pearls and twinset brigade.

The world had changed almost beyond recognition. The full-blown revolution began in Poland in 1989 and continued in Hungary, East Germany, Bulgaria, Czechoslovakia and Romania. One feature common to most of these developments was the extensive use of campaigns of civil resistance, demonstrating popular opposition to the continuation of one-party rule and contributing to the pressure for change. Romania was the only Eastern Bloc country whose people overthrew its Communist regime violently.

Protests in Tiananmen Square (April to June 1989) failed to stimulate major political changes in China, but influential images of courageous defiance during that protest helped to precipitate events in other parts of the globe. On 4 June 1989 the trade union Solidarity won an overwhelming victory in a partially free election in Poland, leading to the peaceful fall of Communism in that country in the summer of 1989.

Hungary began (June 1989) dismantling its section of the physical Iron Curtain, leading to a mass exodus of East Germans through Hungary, which destabilised East Germany. This led to mass demonstrations in cities such as Leipzig and subsequently to the fall of the Berlin Wall in November 1989, which served as the symbolic gateway to German reunification in 1990.

The Soviet Union dissolved in December 1991, resulting in 11 new countries (Armenia, Azerbaijan, Belarus, Georgia, Kazakhstan, Kyrgyzstan, Moldova, Tajikistan, Turkmenistan, Ukraine and Uzbekistan) which had declared their independence from the Soviet Union in the course of the year, while the Baltic states (Estonia, Latvia and Lithuania) regained their independence. The rest of the Soviet Union, which constituted the bulk of the area, became the Russian Federation in December 1991.

Albania and Yugoslavia abandoned Communism between 1990 and 1992. By 1992, Yugoslavia had split into five successor states: Bosnia and Herzegovina, Croatia, Macedonia, Slovenia and the Federal Republic of Yugoslavia, which was later renamed Serbia and Montenegro in 2003 and eventually split into two states, Serbia and Montenegro, in 2006. Serbia was then further split with the breakaway of the partially recognised state of Kosovo in 2008.

Czechoslovakia dissolved three years after the end of Communist rule, splitting peacefully into the Czech Republic and Slovakia in 1992. The impact of these events made itself felt in several Socialist countries. Communism was abandoned in countries such as Cambodia(1991), Ethiopia (1990), Mongolia (which in 1990 democratically re-elected a Communist government that ran the country until 1996) and South Yemen (1990).

Josie reflected on the youngsters today who wanted to be footballers or appear on reality or talent tv shows as an easy fix to getting rich and famous. Girl stars appeared in little more than underwear or beach wear as they slid their lithe young bodies pornographic poses leaving little to the imagination. These airbrushed heavily painted females were role models for countless little girls who could never be thin enough or perfect enough. The sad part was that most of them were interchangeable, there were blonde versions and brunette, Barbies with short spans in the media then they vanished without trace.

Cyber bullying on line also undermined confidence. Innocence seems to disappear earlier than ever before. Josie was reminiscing with her friends about wearing liberty bodices growing up, boys wore short pants to school in all weather. TV had 3 stations with a screen saver little girl card testing picture during the day. People rented televisions, so maintenance was covered, and the sets could be changed when outdated. Those days seemed so innocent and pure compared to the modern era.

There was a constant fear of terrorist attacks, nowhere was safe. Innocent people going about their business were killed because they happened to be in the wrong place at the time. They could be relaxing on a beach holiday, going shopping or at a concert. Wars were still taking place. Discrimination and prejudice was still raising its ugly head. Gender barriers were liberal in most countries, religion and preconceived ethnic prejudices still prevailed. Sex attackers, paedophiles and groomers of youngsters also featured regularly in the news. Children were not safe to play out unsupervised. Girls from poor countries were tricked into sex slave prostitution. With all the modern developments, the world had not improved.

Eleanor and Josie went on several National Express coach trips feeling young. Vicky also went with Josie a few times. They found the trips to be good value and it was relaxing to let the driver take over. It was a good way to explore the UK. Annually, Eleanor and Josie went abroad for beach holidays and adventures, going to America one year to visit friends. They tried to go to different places and keep learning. Once a year Eleanor, Vicky, Aimee and Josie had a long weekend away in Bridlington, on the Yorkshire coast, where they went to top name shows, relaxed, viewed the changes and felt like it was their second home.

Chiara and Ben moved to a bigger house which they renovated designer style over the years. Their children had busy social diaries always rushing to activities or parties. A few years later Elise and Alessandro also moved to a bigger house. Their children were also busy. All the boys enjoyed football and were on teams. Olivia had grown up surrounded by boys, so apart from enjoying girlie clothes, she was unfamiliar with dolls and prams. They were all very close and stayed with Josie one day a week during the school holidays.

Life was busy, fast moving and Josie suddenly sat up startled. She was supposed to call in at the school to renew her security pass, she had forgotten to do it yesterday. The road works had diverted her and now it was too late as the office only opened at set times. Shaking herself in annoyance, Josie thought "I can't sit here dreaming all day. I need to get going, the kids will need collecting soon."

Josie jumped up and rushed out of the house.

end

26754928R00043

Printed in Poland
by Amazon Fulfillment
Poland Sp. z o.o., Wrocław